THE SEA *of* TRANQUILITY

On 16th July 1969 the Apollo 11 mission was launched
from Cape Canaveral, U.S.A. Neil Armstrong, Edwin 'Buz' Aldrin
and Michael Collins were the American astronauts chosen for the
first moon landing. On 20th July 1969 Armstrong and Aldrin stepped
out of the lunar module and walked across the dusty surface of the
Sea of Tranquility. History was made.

Other books from Collins illustrated by Christian Birmingham:

The Magical Bicycle by Berlie Doherty
Windhover by Alan Brown
Oliver Twist by Charles Dickens

First published in hardback in Great Britain by HarperCollins Publishers Ltd in 1996
First published in Picture Lions in 1997
5 7 9 10 8 6 4
ISBN: 0 00 664557 7
Picture Lions is an imprint of the Children's Division, part of HarperCollins Publishers Ltd.
Text copyright © Mark Haddon 1996
Illustrations copyright © Christian Birmingham 1996
The author and illustrator assert the moral right to be identified as the author and illustrator of the work.
A CIP catalogue record for this title is available from the British Library.
Printed and bound in Italy.

THE SEA *of* TRANQUILITY

The Sea of Tranquility

Mark Haddon
Illustrated by Christian Birmingham

PictureLions
An Imprint of HarperCollinsPublishers

Years ago
there was a little boy
who had the solar system on his wall.

Late at night, he'd lie in bed
with Rabbit
and they'd watch the planets
spinning round the sun:
Mars, the tiny space-tomato,
Saturn, sitting in its Frisbee rings,
freezing Pluto, turning slowly in the dark,
Jupiter, Uranus, Neptune, Venus, Mercury
and Earth.

But of all the weird worlds
that whirled across his bedroom wall,
his favourite was the moon,
a small and bald and ordinary
globe of rock
that loop-the-looped
its way through outer space.

He leant across the windowsill at night
and watched the moon slide up into the sky
above the biscuit factory.

He borrowed Dad's binoculars
and gazed for hours
at the empty deserts
and the rocky mountains.

And it made him dizzy
just to think that he was looking
at another world
two hundred thousand miles away.

He got an atlas of the moon
for Christmas
and he read it
like a storybook.

He dreamed of going there,
of rocketing across the cold, black miles,
and landing on the crumbly rock.
He dreamed of visiting
the craters in the atlas,
Prosper Henry, Klaproth, Zack.
He dreamed of driving
in a fat-tyred moon-mobile,
across the Bay of Rainbows
and the Sea of Rains…

He kept a scrapbook called *The Journey to the Moon*.
Inside were photographs of rockets
taking off from Cape Canaveral
and astronauts in pumped-up suits
and fishbowl helmets,
floating in the zero gravity
around their little metal rooms.

He borrowed library books
and read how astronauts
had orbited the earth
and walked in space,
and how they'd flown around the moon itself.
And every night he hoped and hoped
that one day they would find a way to land
and walk across the tiny world
where he had dreamed of walking.

And eventually, one cloudless night,
they did.

He couldn't sleep.
Midnight had come and gone,
but he was wide awake
and standing at the window
in his dressing gown,
because two astronauts
were walking on the surface of the moon,
two hundred thousand miles
above his bedroom.

At 3 a.m.
he went downstairs
and turned the television on.
And there they were,
on the flickery screen,
bouncing slowly through the dust
in the Sea of Tranquility,
like giants in slow motion.

He stayed awake all night
and went to bed at dawn.
The sun was coming up
outside his window
and the moon was fading fast.
He fell asleep
and in his dreams
he walked with them.